Dear Reader,

The research contained within these pages is confidential.
If you have one of our rare journals in your possession,
you should consider it a privilege.

We at The Society of Magbeologists have made it
our life's mission to preserve, protect and facilitate the
continued survival of magic-kind species.

If you would like to join our cause, and have a great
reverence for life (and a bit of mystery) then please do
read on. If not, I dare say you should return this journal
immediately from where you found it.

Magbeology is a serious scientific field – and we wish
to only recruit those as fascinated by the world of
magic as we are.

Best Wishes,
Dr. Abram Fitzgerald
Head of Environmental Department

The Society of
Magbeologists

established in 1852

~ Quest ~
for the
Dragon Stone

red
cygnet™
P R E S S

To Lance,
for always believing and keeping me dreaming.

To Destiny,
for allowing me to see life through the innocent eyes of a child.
– A.B.

Illustrations copyright © 2007 Ami Blackford
Manuscript copyright © 2007 Ami Blackford
Book copyright © 2007 Red Cygnet Press, Inc., 11858 Stoney Peak Dr. #525,
San Diego, CA 92128

Cover and book design: Amy Stirnkorb

First Edition 2007
10 9 8 7 6 5 4 3 2
Printed in China

Library of Congress Cataloging-in-Publication Data
is available at our website: www.redcygnet.com

~ Quest ~
for the
Dragon Stone

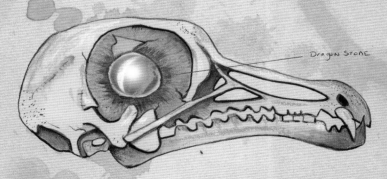

DRAGON STONE

Written and Illustrated by

Ami Blackford

CONFIDENTIAL

A DUNCAN FAMILY ADVENTURE

red cygnet™
PRESS

San Diego, California

"What are we going to do?" Ruth Duncan tilted back in her battered chair, her slender fingers drumming on the desk. A beeswax candle burned brightly, washing her work space in soft light. David, her older brother, rolled his eyes while flipping through his sketchbook.

"*We?* I don't want any part in this."

"You really aren't even interested in seeing him?" asked Ruth, staring absently at the neatly printed observations in her field journal. It had been a rewarding day—her fieldwork more exciting than usual.

"Nope. I'm done with it," David pushed back his baseball cap, exposing his spiky blonde hair. "So, quit

nagging me." Ruth sighed heavily. She knew when to leave her big brother alone. Gazing out her open bedroom window, she thought of the mysterious species occupying her surroundings at Cottonwood.

Only a true Magbeologist—one dedicated to the study of magical beasts—knew such creatures existed. A sudden flicker of light outside the window and the whisper of wings announced the arrival of Simone, Cottonwood cottage's resident faerie. Simone had occupied the cottage for more than one hundred years.

"You are relentless!" Simone wagged a tiny finger as she buzzed around the desk.

"Relentless. Dedicated. Genius," Ruth stretched like a satisfied cat. "Call it what you like."

Simone crossed her arms while rolling her eyes.

"How about adding a few.... like bigheaded—perhaps even pretentious?" David stifled a laugh. He continued sketching, ignoring the faerie.

Ruth gave David a light kick on his shin, while Simone took a quick survey of the bedroom. "Where did you put him?"

Simone landed atop Ruth's open journal, her tiny feet crushing a rare collection of faerie wings. Ruth nudged Simone carefully aside with the tip of her finger. "Please, it took an entire summer to collect these molted wings," Ruth snipped.

"Sorry," grumbled Simone, shoving a strand of short black hair back inside her velvet hat. She scooted off the journal and onto the desk. "—you still haven't answered my question."

Ruth huffed loudly, then slumped forward and cradled her face in her palms. Through a jumble of fingers she mumbled, "You're going to think I'm a lunatic."

"I *already* think you're a lunatic—you are a Duncan after all." Simone possessed the annoying tendency to be equally as relentless as Ruth. It was quite possibly one reason they got along so well. Simone shot David a sideways glance as he pretended to ignore them.

Ruth pivoted in her chair, casting a quick look at her closed bedroom door. Being a very serious and dedicated Magbeologist—and only eleven years old—still meant she had others to consider. Her mother didn't tolerate discussion of anything magical, fanciful—or fun, for that matter. She was a very serious woman, an English literature professor at the nearby community college.

"He's in the barn," Ruth said cautiously. The Society of Magbeologists had very strict rules about bringing work home. Ruth was permitted to do her fieldwork and return with nothing more than samples and a

record of her observations—*end of story.* But some days there were exceptions and rules had to be broken.

Today happened to be one of those days.

"What do you plan to do with him?" Simone's amber eyes grew rounder than two shiny pennies. Ruth noted David's pencil slowed as he listened for her response.

"I haven't figured that out quite yet," snapped Ruth, irritated at Simone's prying questions. She had been contemplating her solution when Simone appeared. "I don't even know if he'll survive the night." Ruth pushed aside the thin gossamer curtains billowing in the soft night breeze. She stared anxiously at the old barn, which sat at the edge of the woods.

The barn hadn't housed animals since her father's disappearance five years ago.

Now, it housed one very *large* and very *sick* dragon.

As Ruth observed the dragon earlier this morning in the woods, he appeared to be abnormally weak. She couldn't leave the poor beast vulnerable to the elements. It was the oath she took as a Magbeologist.

After her father's disappearance, Ruth decided to carry on his studies while David had decided to give them up. She knew Samuel Duncan would never leave an injured beast unattended.

And so—neither would Ruth Duncan.

"What kind of dragon is it…. won't the demon catch fire to the place?" Simone was now pacing across Ruth's desk, her hands waving about in an agitated manner. Ruth put on her bottlecap glasses and adjusted them, a frown tugging at the corners of her mouth.

Picking up *Dr. Fitzgerald's Magbeological Guide*, she skimmed the illustrations with a swift finger and whispered, "I believe he's an Aztec Amphithere—also referred to as the Phoenix Dragon. He *is* a fire breather. However, he wasn't doing much more than smoldering when I observed him this afternoon." Ruth sat back with an exhausted sigh. "He came quite peacefully—I just offered him a bit of peacock stew." Setting aside his sketchbook,

David was now peering over Ruth's shoulder at the illustration of the species. He remained silent, which aggravated Ruth.

"You say he's a Phoenix Dragon?" Simone stopped pacing suddenly, her eyes narrowing as she glanced toward the barn.

"Yes, he has all the correct physiology, which is surprising to me since they are native to South America. I am assuming he migrated here for environmental reasons."

Ruth had a finger pressed to the illustration as Simone stepped onto the open page of the reference book. Ruth tilted her head. "Why do you ask?"

Simone bent low, her soft light illuminated the illustration.

"Your father spent years tracking a Phoenix Dragon. It's believed that particular breed carries the legendary Draconite." Simone crawled across the page as she investigated the diagram of the dragon.

Ruth felt a sharp pain at the mention of her father's name.

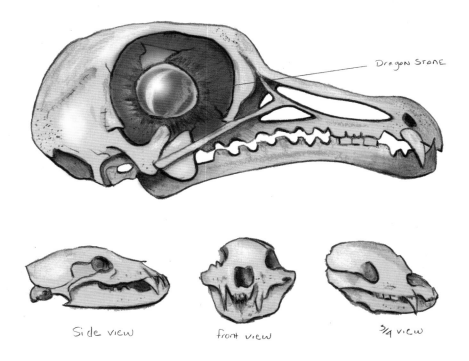

Dragon Stone

Side view   front view   ¾ view

David finally broke his oath of silence, "What a bunch of hogwash!" He had promised himself over a year ago never to study or interact with any magic-kind species, but this discussion had grown intolerable.

Simone stood on the desk, her face tilted defiantly up toward David. "Oh, *now* Mr. Fancy Pants is going to speak to me?"

Twirling her blonde hair into a bun, Ruth stuck two pencils through the thick wad. "There is no proof that a Dragon Stone exists. One has never been found," said Ruth, trying to diffuse the argument that had erupted.

"Just because you haven't seen it, doesn't mean it doesn't exist!" Simone's face flushed redder than a summer strawberry. She flew off the desk, hovering only inches from Ruth's face.

"Just because you believe in something doesn't make it real!" David barked loudly. Simone turned toward him, her wings flapping as swiftly as a hummingbird's.

Great, Ruth thought. *Now Simone is mad.* Although faeries were small, Ruth had learned years ago they could cause quite a ruckus when agitated.

"I will believe in the Dragon Stone when I see a Dragon Stone." said Ruth. She swore she saw smoke shoot out of Simone's pointy ears, as the faerie turned angrily toward her.

"Your father would be horrified to hear both of you say such things!" Simone barked while jamming a small finger into the fleshy tip of Ruth's nose. "He

Proper Procedure for Appeasing an Angry Faerie

1. Avoid direct eye contact. An angered faerie has magical iris properties which may bend you to their whim.
2. Do not argue with a faerie - no matter the temptation. Simply conceed to disagree.
3. Offer a token of apology. Faeries love to be given gifts. Some favorites include: Shiny pennies, turquoise, rose quartz and shells from the ocean.

Dr.Fitzgerald's Magbeological Guide : A Scientific Resource Book of Magical Beasts
Excerpt taken from Chapter 10: Faerie Relations

believed in the Dragon Stone!" Simone hovered nose to nose with Ruth, her dark brows knit fiercely.

"Well, he can't hear us… because he's never come home." David's voice faltered only a second before he added, "And, he wasted his life chasing fantasies."

"I evaluate research—cold, hard facts," said Ruth sadly. She was tired of arguing. Grabbing her back-pack, Ruth walked softly toward the bedroom door. The old hinges creaked as she nudged it open.

Slowly, Ruth stuck her head out into the hall. Simone landed gently on her shoulder. "What are you doing?"

"Before I answer that…are you done yelling at us?"

Simone shrugged her slender shoulders. "For now, I suppose."

Ruth poked her head back in the room. "I am making certain we don't get caught."

"Get caught doing what?"

"Sneaking out to the barn," replied Ruth. She grabbed her field journal and flagged Simone to follow her out into the hall.

David hesitated in the doorway.

"Come on," whispered Ruth, looking back at her brother. "There's only one way to find out if Dad's theory of the existence of the Dragon Stone is valid."

"*You* can examine the Phoenix Dragon," David snorted. He grabbed his sketchbook and joined them in the hall. "I'll come along, but I still don't want any part in this."

Simone snorted in response.

Ruth smiled. "You've got a deal."

Ruth and David stood in the gaping doorway, purple and black shadow cloaked the barn's interior. A sliver of moonlight splashed the dirt floor, revealing a large lumpy silhouette curled in a ball just beyond the threshold. As Simone flew toward the beast, her golden light filled the damp barn. "He's awfully young to be so sick."

"He's been in and out of consciousness all day," Ruth whispered. She struck a match and ignited the lantern hanging by the door. The old wick sputtered before bursting into hot flame. David held the lantern high, illuminating the slumbering dragon. He was three times the size of a cow with red and orange fur covering his well-muscled frame.

The Phoenix Dragon had large feathery wings. His legs and arms were tucked neatly beneath his body. A crown of fiery colored feathers decorated his head. Ruth thought he was magnificent and wondered if she should give him a name.

"He didn't eat his dinner." Ruth picked up the untouched plate of lamb chops lying on the ground.

"This dragon is definitely sick," said David with concern. He hated to admit it, but he had missed interacting with magic-kind.

"I need to examine him." Ruth walked to the small desk located to the right of the open door, and lifted a small leather satchel from one of the drawers. Setting the satchel on the ground, she proceeded to extract her exami-

nation tools.

"There is

something I

need to discuss

with you both," said Simone,

while Ruth carefully set out

a Dragoscope, an Internal

Magnifying Glass, nostril plugs, and one sample jar.

David sat and began sketching the dragon. He didn't

want to participate in examining him—but he did

want to draw the beast.

"I'm listening," Ruth began carefully cleaning the

Dragoscope and Internal Magnifying Glass with a soft

cloth.

Simone crawled atop the sample jar and shot David

a look.

"What?" said David. "I'm listening—no more

silent treatment, I promise." Simone nodded, accept-

ing the treaty between them. It had been over a year

since he had spoken to her.

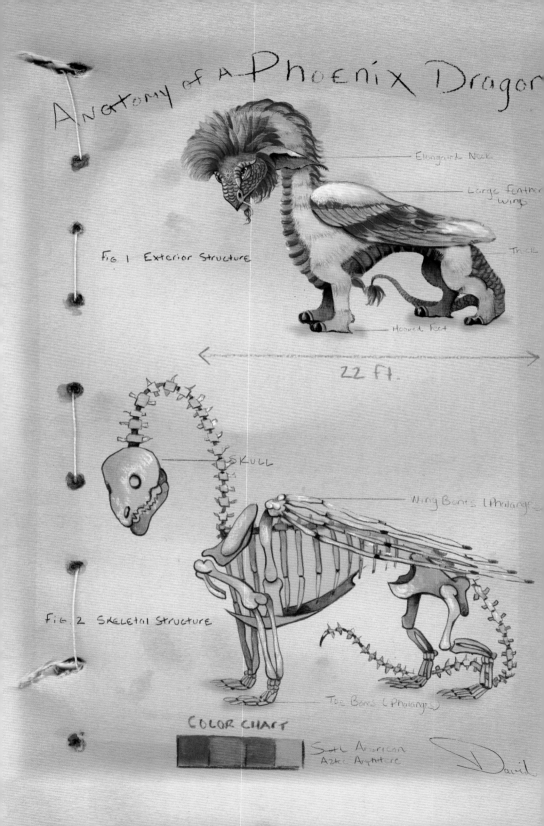

Anatomy of a Phoenix Dragon

Elongated Neck

Large Feather Wings

Fig. 1 Exterior Structure

Thick

Hooved Feet

22 Ft.

SKULL

Wing Bones (Phalanges)

Fig. 2 Skeletal Structure

Toe Bones (Phalanges)

COLOR CHART

S. American
Aztec Amphitere

David

"Your father Samuel spent years seeking a Phoenix Dragon for the sole purpose of locating a Dragon Stone. It was the last piece he needed to finalize his research of the Twelve Ancient Relics of Alchemy. The Dragon Stone was the only relic he couldn't locate." Simone began fiddling with the large opal button fastened to the front of her wool shawl.

"He didn't talk much about his research—" said Ruth, hanging the Dragoscope around her neck and fitting the earpieces snuggly into place. "Dad was *very* private about his work." Ruth swallowed hard before turning to David, "Did you know about this?" Ruth still held onto the hope someday her dad might show up at the cottage with a wild tale of his expeditions.

"I knew some of the details," replied David.

Simone paused and took a deep breath. "A special group at the Society has been recording disturbances in the environment, and the concerns this raises in reference to magic-kind. Samuel was part of a specialty team investigating the Ancient Relics of Alchemy as a solution." Simone's voice softened to a whisper.

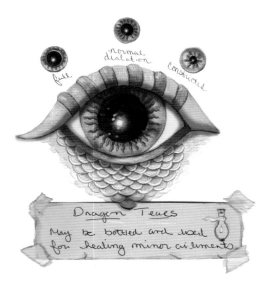

"A solution to what?" Ruth stopped working. All of a sudden, she did *not* like the sound of all this. Neither did David. He disregarded his drawing and moved toward them.

Simone answered. "To some future problems that have been predicted."

Ruth lifted back the scaly eyelids of the Phoenix Dragon. Pointing her tiny flashlight in his eyes, she observed they were fully dilated.

He was in hibernation, the first stage of expiration.

"What kind of *problems*?" asked David and Ruth in unison.

Simone fell silent. She signaled that she needed a moment.

Stages of Expiration

Stage 1

Hibernation

Stage 2

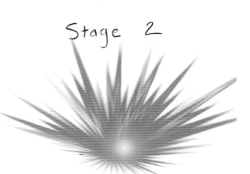

Combustion

Stage 3

Decomposition

Stage 4

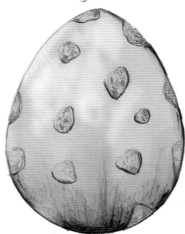

Rebirth

Ruth reached for the nostril plugs.

"You don't need those," said David. A thin tendril of smoke escaped the dragon's nostrils. "Clearly his fire-breathing reflex has a blockage obstructing the canal between his poison reservoir and ignition pouch."

Simone cleared her throat, indicating she was ready to answer their question.

"Doctor Fitzgerald's team predicts mass extinction," Simone blurted. She met Ruth and David's horrified expressions, her amber eyes watery with tears.

"Magic-kind faces *extinction?*" It was a horrible word—a word no scientist ever wanted to hear. Ruth circled the dragon, trying hard to decide how she would lift his chin and use the Dragoscope at the same time. Without a word, David got behind the dragon, and with all his strength lifted its large head. His eyes bulged as he strained to hold the beast's head upright and steady.

"They must be wrong," said Ruth, thankful for David's assistance. Placing the steel surface of the Drag-oscope against the fleshy underside of the dragon's

throat, she heard a wheeze and rattle within. A healthy dragon should produce a solid rumble—definitely not a wheezing rattle.

"The prediction has already begun to come true," said Simone. "Look at this dragon! A Phoenix Dragon of this age is too young to be in expiration."

Ruth looked up at David. "You can set him down."

"You took long enough!" groaned David. He gently eased the dragon's head back to the nest of straw. Sweat poured down his forehead as he moved toward Ruth.

"Here, you examine his head if you think you are so much quicker," snapped Ruth as she handed David the Internal Magnifying Glass.

He hesitated for only a moment. "No harm in that, I suppose," said David. He took the device and moved with expert precision around the dragon's cranium. As David examined the internal workings of the brain, Ruth's mind raced frantically. "How are the magic relics the solution?" asked Ruth, peeking over David's shoulder at the blue flesh of the dragon's brain. It pulsed with life beneath the X-ray properties of the magnifying glass.

Brain of a Phoenix Dragon

energy Molecules

Regenerative
Brain tissue

Crown feather
from Phoenix
Dragon

Ruth

It was written in *Dr. Fitzgerald's Magbeological Guide* that Draconite was located within the brain of the dragon.

"Eleven years ago, Samuel excavated an ancient wheel while on a dig in Africa," Simone explained. "When he returned to the Society with it, he discovered it was a relic left by the ancestors of magic-kind. The legend is that when all the relics are placed upon the wheel, a message left by the ancestors will reveal information pertinent to the continued survival of our species."

"You mean he spent our entire life tracking the relics?" Ruth asked heatedly. David chimed in. "Yes, when I was three and you had just been born, he told Mom he had to go on this quest." David moved around the beast's head, searching desperately for the fabled Dragon Stone. "He came back from time to time, but never for long."

"He was determined to find all the relics," Simone added as she flew around David fretfully. The dragon didn't stir—but his body began to glow brightly.

Last

Ruth & David,
the Targeta forest
is amazing - filled
with Illumina-
Nympa Species.
Here I am
surrounded by them
while c...

Ruth & David Duncan
410 Cottonwood Drive
Cottonwood, GA 32106

Contact
with
Dad

David   Ruth

The light filled the barn. David continued his search, knowing the fiery glow signaled the dragon was in Stage Two, combustion. After hunting and probing the entire skull, David stood swiftly and took Ruth by the arm.

"If the Dragon Stone exists—it's not in this dragon." David nudged Ruth backward as the dragon glowed brighter. "You might want to shield your eyes."

Ruth knew what was about to happen.

Suddenly, the Phoenix Dragon burst into a ball of hot flame. The beast disintegrated into a mound of ash, completing Stage Three—decomposition.

Simone gasped as ashes drifted down around them, falling softly to the packed-earth floor. "The description of this species' unusual expiration in Dr. Fitzgerald's guide certainly did not do such a spectacle justice," said Ruth. She was seized with disappointment and a touch of sadness. "I never had the opportunity to name him." After taking several snapshots of the ashy mound with her camera, David patted her gently on the shoulder. "It's for the best; you know the number one rule of Magbeology is to—"

"—never get personally involved with your studies," said Ruth, finishing his sentence. Sometimes that was a hard rule to follow.

Ruth returned to her satchel and retrieved a pair of sample collectors. She approached the decomposition site gingerly as she tried to decide where to crouch for the sample.

"Try to get some ash from the very center of the pile," said David. "Why am I always the one to do the dirty work?" grumbled Ruth under her breath. Using the sample collectors, she scooped up a healthy portion of dragon ash.

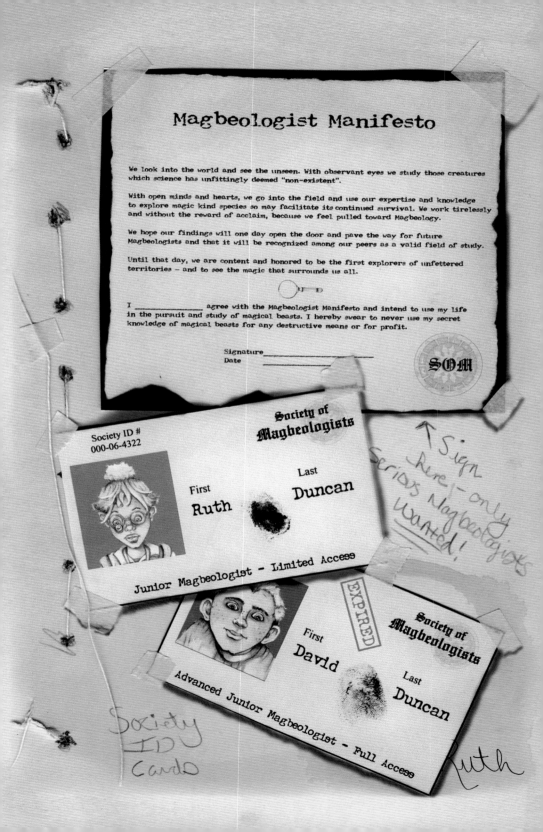

"It would be ironic if the dragon your father chased across the globe ended up on your back doorstep," said Simone.

Carefully, Ruth unscrewed the cap of the jar and poised the collectors over the rim. Dragon ash smeared across the bridge of her nose as she spoke. "One thing I have learned, Simone, is *nothing* can be that ironic." As Ruth dumped the soot into the jar, she and Simone jumped at the loud *clank* that resonated in the silence of the barn. David hurried over to look in the jar.

Peering at Simone over the edge of her glasses, Ruth said, "You know the probability of that being the Dragon Stone is very low." She let her gaze drift to the bottom of the jar—grayish-black ash filled it, obscuring her view. "Nearly impossible," added David, his heart racing with excitement.

"You want to bet?" whispered Simone. She flew to the rim of the jar, and poked her nose into the ashy interior. "It would make sense that the two of you would find it."

"Why is that?" asked Ruth. She looked a mess. Her

hair bun hung lopsided—the pencils drooping to touch her ears. She had dragon soot smeared across her forehead, nose, and glasses.

"Because, only a pair of Duncans are fit for such a crazy discovery."

"How flattering," said Ruth, pushing a stray piece of hair from her eyes.

"It's probably just a fragment of bone…there is a logical explanation, I'm sure," said David. Ruth picked up the lantern at her feet and crossed the barn to her desk. She set the lantern down. The soft light washed the dusty mahogany wood in uneven waves as the flame flickered high and then low.

"I'll make a deal with you guys," said Simone excitedly. "If that is indeed the Dragon Stone, you will pick up where Samuel left off."

Ruth arched a brow as she pulled on a pair of latex gloves. She looked at David. He shrugged. Setting out an empty collection pan, Ruth prepared to dump the sample in the tin. "And—if *we* are right, and it's nothing more than a left-over remnant of the dragon…."

ashes from Phoenix Dragon

David

STAGE 3

Decomposition of a Phoenix Dragon

1. When Phoenix Dragon begins to emanate magic-light after a period of Hibernation - step back a safe distance and shield eyes. Combustion is very bright.
2. Once Combustion has taken place - wait approximately 10-15 minutes for dragon ash to cool. Temperatures have been recorded as high as 200 degrees.
3. Make certain to retrieve the newly formed Phoenix Dragon egg from ashes and prepare for Rebirth Approximate hatching time: 14 months.

Dr.Fitzgerald's Magbeological Guide: Scientific Resource Book of Magical Beasts
Excerpt taken from Chapter 3 : Aztec Amphithere

"Then—I will snitch out every magical beast in Cottonwood so you might observe them to your Magbeologist's heart's content!"

"That is quite an offer," said David.

"An offer I can't refuse," said Ruth. "You have a deal." Ruth slowly poured the contents of the jar into the pan. Something large rolled out from the soot. Using her gloved fingertips, Ruth swiftly brushed aside the ash. Hunkered over the pan, Ruth rubbed the object clean while Simone and David waited impatiently behind her.

Several excruciating moments passed. "The suspense is driving me mad," snapped David. "Is it the Dragon Stone or isn't it?"

"I suppose there is only one thing left to say," grumbled Ruth dryly.

"What is that?" asked Simone.

"Where exactly did our father leave off?" Ruth turned slowly, unfolding her gloved palm to reveal the sacred Draconite. It gleamed like a freshly excavated pearl from the fleshy confines of an oyster.

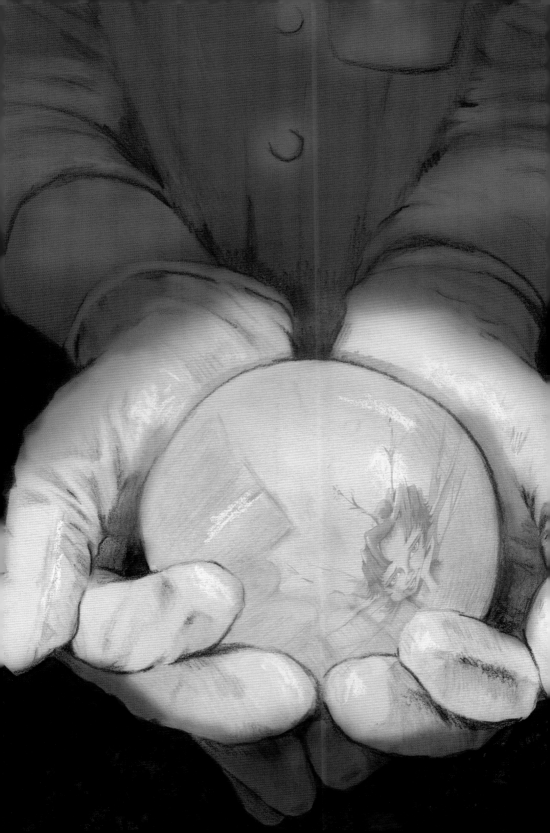

"I don't believe it," said David, his mouth gaping.

"Just because you don't believe in something doesn't mean it doesn't exist," said Simone, sitting cross-legged on top of the old desk.

Ruth approached the pile of ash. "What are you doing?" asked David. "Stage Four, rebirth, should be complete," said Ruth. She knew that an egg housing a baby Phoenix Dragon would be waiting in the ash. Phoenix Dragons never actually died. The dragons were simply reborn within their own ashes. They would need to bring the egg to the Society for proper hatching.

"What do we do next?" asked David.

Simone chimed in. "He'll explain it all. In the bottom drawer, on page 42 of his *Huckleberry Finn* novel is a letter that has been waiting for you both."

As Ruth sifted through the ash, her hands hit the egg. It was still hot. Delicately, she brushed off the ash and wrapped it in a towel.

"A letter from whom?" asked David. Ruth gently placed the egg in her book bag next to the jar that held the Dragon Stone.

"Samuel told me when he left five years ago, if he didn't return by December this year, I should lead you to the letter."

"It's March," snapped Ruth, her heart hammering.

Simone tapped the desk with her foot.

"I thought I'd give him a few extra months!"

David pulled the bottom drawer open. A spider crawled out of the darkness within.

"Look on the bright side, guys," Simone smiled, "Draconite is one of the Twelve Relics."

"So?" mumbled Ruth, while David sifted through the pile of books in the drawer. "Now, we only have to retrieve eleven more."

Grabbing the dusty copy of *Huckleberry Finn* crammed in the bottom drawer, David felt his pulse quicken. Before opening the book, he looked up at Ruth. "Well, this day has been filled with surprises."

As David located the yellowed envelope sandwiched in the pages, Ruth moved closer. "Yeah, and from the looks of it—things are just getting started."

Ruth and David waited nervously in Dr. Abram Fitzgerald's office, with their father's letter in hand. He had been surprised to see them at headquarters and he escorted them quickly into his stuffy office. The room was crammed with piles of books, paperwork, and exotic antiquities. They heard a loud cough and scuffle before he came through the door.

"It's a surprise to see you both. I had expected a call sooner." The old Magbeologist coughed loudly, his bushy white hair shaking with the movement.

"We just got Dad's letter," said David. Dr. Fitzgerald set his watery green eyes on them, his crooked nose was red and irritated. "Yes, well what brings you here so late…your mother will be worried."

"We needed to deliver this for proper hatching." Ruth carefully opened her knapsack and handed the red-orange spotted egg to the doctor. Squinting, he examined it.

"Good heavens! This looks like—" He grabbed his bifocals and quickly shoved them on his face. "—The egg of a Phoenix Dragon." Dr. Fitzgerald set his finger to a red button on his phone.

"We had a young Phoenix Dragon expire in our barn today," replied David. A woman in a long white laboratory coat suddenly appeared. With gloved palms, she scooped up the egg without as much as a glance their way.

"We'll put him in the hatchery—he's in good hands," Dr. Fitzgerald whispered.

"The egg isn't the only thing we have to deliver," said Ruth, reaching back inside her backpack. The doctor sneezed loudly and sat forward. "What else did you bring?"

"Something you've been searching for," said Ruth. She produced the jar from her backpack. Dr. Fitzgerald raised his bushy white brows and gasped when Ruth passed the jar to David.

"Is that the—" The old doctor fumbled for the jar as David passed it to him. "It is. The Dragon Stone," said David. Dr. Fitzgerald opened the jar and held the magic relic in the soft light of his lamp. Ruth cleared her throat.

"We are here to continue our father's expedition and excavate the remaining Relics of Alchemy." Dr. Fitzgerald stopped his examination of the Dragon Stone. His eyes set hard on Ruth and David.

"It's good to hear you say that." He sighed heavily before adding, "The prevention of magic-kind's extinction depends on the continuation of your father's work. When Samuel disappeared, our Relics of Alchemy team became disenchanted with the project. They were all too frightened to carry on."

"Too frightened?" asked Ruth.

"Yes. There are many leaders in magic-kind who do not support our Extinction Theory. Your father had no troubles locating the relics, but he said getting the relics relinquished for our research would be difficult." Abram blew his nose loudly.

"Dad disappeared once he began trying to excavate the relics," said David. It all made sense to him now.

Ancient Relics
of
Alchemy Wheel

Top Secret!

Society Daily News

March 13th, 2006
DRAGON STONE HAS BEEN LOCATED!

I am excited to report that Ruth and David Duncan,
children of our late Samuel Duncan, have discovered
the illusive Draconite after a young Phoenix Dragon
expired in their barn. They have delivered both the
relic and the Phoenix Egg to me. I am pleased to
announce that the Ancient Relics of Alchemy Expeditions
are officially re-instated. Volunteers are needed.
— Dr. Abram Fitzgerald

Ruth

"That is correct," Dr. Fitzgerald answered. "I would have carried on this project, however—" Another loud round of coughs filled the room before the old man added "—I have taken ill and I'm much too old for such a dangerous mission."

Ruth and David stared at each other. They were Duncans and they knew this is what their father wanted.

"Are you ready to continue your father's quest?" Dr. Fitzgerald asked.

David smiled at Ruth. "We are ready."

Ruth smiled at David. He had used the word *we*.

Together, she knew they were ready for anything.

To My dearest David and Ruthie,

December 20th, 1999

If you are directed to read this letter, then five years will have passed since I have been home. Regretfully, if that much time has passed with no word from me, I would have to say it would be safe to assume something went wrong while I was out in the field.

I have never disclosed to you my research and why I spent so many years traveling the world and not at home with you and Mommy. It is my hope that if I am gone, you both will carry on my work and facilitate the Society in finalizing this research project.

Doctor Fitzgerald from the Society will be expecting a phone call from you no later than April 2004. He has all of my documentations and will disclose the entire project to you in person.

You may reach him at 590-621-1410 Ex. 32

Enclosed is the feather from the tail of a rare Icelandic peacock. You may use this to lure a dragon. Peacock is one of their favorite meats.

I love you Ruthie and David. I only wish now I had spent more time with you, rather than hunting the world for ancient relics.

Keep up your studies.
Through our work we may always be together.

Love,

Dad